**First published in Canada and the United States in 2019**
Text copyright © 2019 Jane Whittingham
Illustration copyright © 2019 Emma Pedersen
This edition copyright © 2019 Pajama Press Inc.
This is a first edition.

10 9 8 7 6 5 4 3 2 1

The publisher gratefully acknowledges the support of the Canada Council for the Arts and the Ontario Arts Council for its publishing program. We acknowledge the financial support of the Government of Canada through the Canada Book Fund (CBF) for our publishing activities.

**Library and Archives Canada Cataloguing in Publication**

Whittingham, Jane, 1984-, author
        Queenie Quail can't keep up / by Jane Whittingham ; illustrated
by Emma Pedersen. -- First edition.
ISBN 978-1-77278-067-3 (hardcover)
        I. Pedersen, Emma, 1988-, illustrator  II. Title.
PS8645.H5695Q44 2019          jC813'.6          C2018-903834-9

**Publisher Cataloging-in-Publication Data (U.S.)**

Names: Whittingham, Jane, 1984-, author. | Pedersen, Emma, illustrator.
Title: Queenie Quail Can't Keep Up / by Jane Whittingham ; illustrated by Emma Pedersen.
Description: Toronto, Ontario Canada : Pajama Press, 2018. | Summary: "Busy observing the world, Queenie Quail is often admonished to keep up with her parents and nine siblings. When Queenie's watchful eye spots a cat in the grass, she rescues her family from danger and teaches them the value of slowing down" -- Provided by publisher.
Identifiers: ISBN 978-1-77278-067-3 (hardcover)
Subjects: LCSH: Families – Juvenile fiction. | Birds – Juvenile fiction. | Humorous stories. | BISAC: JUVENILE FICTION / Social Themes / Self-Esteem & Self-Reliance. | JUVENILE FICTION / Social Themes / New Experience.
Classification: LCC PZ7.W558Qu | DDC [E] – dc23

Original art created with gouache
Cover and book design—Rebecca Bender

Manufactured by Qualibre Inc./Printplus
Printed in China

**Pajama Press Inc.**
181 Carlaw Ave. Suite 251 Toronto, Ontario Canada, M4M 2S1

Distributed in Canada by UTP Distribution
5201 Dufferin Street Toronto, Ontario Canada, M3H 5T8

Distributed in the U.S. by Ingram Publisher Services
1 Ingram Blvd. La Vergne, TN 37086, USA

For my dad
—J.W.

For Grandma and Keddy,
for always making me feel at home
—E.P.

Every morning and every evening, Mama Quail led her chicks along the meadow trail, while Papa Quail stood watch from above.

In a straight little line went ten little chicks, and as they went, ten little heads went bob bob bob, ten sets of feet went tap tap tap, and ten round bodies went hurry hurry hurry. But the littlest quail couldn't keep up.

"Queenie Quail, hurry, hurry, hurry!" Mama Quail chirped.

"Hurry, hurry, hurry!" her brothers and sisters cheeped.

"Coming, Mama!" Queenie squeaked.

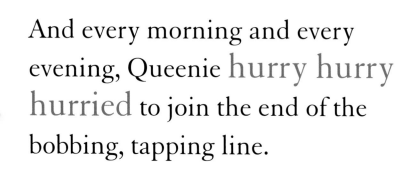

And every morning and every evening, Queenie hurry hurry hurried to join the end of the bobbing, tapping line.

But how could Queenie Quail ever keep up when there were pink blossoms and green grass, shiny stones and fuzzy caterpillars, buzzy bumblebees and wiggly worms?

No matter how hard she tried,
Queenie Quail just couldn't keep up.

"Queenie Quail, you must learn to hurry," Papa Quail chirped. "It is what we quails do!"

"What we do, what we do, what we do!" her brothers and sisters cheeped.

"I'll do my best, Papa," Queenie squeaked.

And really she did.

For days, Queenie bobbed and tapped
and hurry hurry hurried.

But the blossoms were so pink and the grass so green,
the stones so shiny and the caterpillars so fuzzy,
the bumblebees so buzzy and the worms so wiggly,
that no matter how hard she tried, Queenie Quail
just couldn't keep up.

One morning, as Papa Quail stood watch and Mama Quail led her chicks along the meadow trail, Queenie Quail stopped to admire a fascinating feather.

And that's when she saw it.

An unusual flash of orange.

A furry kind of orange.

A **moving** kind of orange.

As Queenie watched, the furry orange slid softly, smoothly, silently through the green grass.

Softly, smoothly, silently, Queenie followed.

Now, Queenie was a curious quail, but she was also a cautious quail. Whatever the furry orange was, Queenie had the uncomfortable feeling that it didn't want to be seen.

The furry orange crept cautiously, carefully, quietly beside the meadow trail.

Cautiously, carefully, quietly, Queenie followed.

Suddenly, through a gap in the green grass, Queenie saw it.

Two pointed ears, two dark eyes, and four paws with sharp claws.

The furry orange was a CAT!

And it was headed straight for Mama Quail and Queenie's brothers and sisters!

There wasn't a moment to lose. Queenie raced along the trail, bobbing, tapping, and hurry, hurry, hurrying. She squeaked and she chirped and she hopped and she flapped.

"A CAT!
A CAT!

Mama!
Papa!

Look out,
look out!"

Papa Quail swooped down from above, flapping and squawking.

Mama Quail raced up the trail, squawking and flapping.

Queenie's brothers and sisters huddled together, chirping and cheeping.

"We see you!

Go away!

Go away, cat!

Go away!"

The cat hissed and snarled.
Then off into the grass it ran
like a furry orange blur.

"You've saved us, Queenie Quail!" Mama Quail chirped.

"Well done, Queenie Quail!" Papa Quail chirped.

"Well done, well done, well done!" her brothers
and sisters cheeped.

Now, every morning and every evening, Mama Quail leads her chicks along the meadow trail while Papa Quail watches over them from above.

In a straight little line go ten little chicks, and as they go, ten little heads go bob bob bob, ten sets of feet go tap tap tap, and ten round bodies go hurry hurry hurry.

But Queenie, the littlest quail, can't keep up.

"Queenie Quail, what have you found?"
Mama Quail chirps.

"What have you found, what
have you found, what have you
found?" her brothers and sisters cheep.

"Something fascinating!" Queenie squeaks,
and her brothers and sisters scurry along
the trail to see.

And that's why Queenie Quail
and her brothers
and her sisters
can't keep up.